the fragile humans we are

volume one

the fragile humans we are

volume one

V. Walker

VW Publishing

Published by VW Publishing
www.vwpublishing.com

ISBN: 979-8-218-57380-5

to the questions that we ask
and never get answered

to the daughters who hate
seeing their mother in the mirror

to the sons who bear
burdens beyond compare

to the children
who never had a chance

and to you, my dear,
the one who is still here.

Contents

trigger warnings

some of the poems reference the following topics:

abuse (**no** graphic descriptions), depression, and grief.

coming of age lessons on love

she is spirit

Sunken cheeks,
bruised body,
lips that utter icy words.
Broken bones,
blackened heart,
fine lines
– one for each man that tore you.

Took your body,
stole your money,
left you in the street.
Yet, here you are with that silly smile on your cracked lips,
they can never take your spirit.

father

We shall give, says father
We may not have a lot of money
But they have no money

We shall give, says father
We may not have nice clothes
But they have no clothes

We shall give, says father
We may not have much food
But they have no food

We shall give, says father
We may not have light
But we can light the path for those in the dark.

solitude, sanity, sacrifice

Solitude:
Sometimes you knock on the door
and I pretend to be asleep.
It's not personal,
But I have
Privacy, locked memories, and secrets
I must keep,
For only me.

Sanity:
Sometimes I force myself back to sleep.
I force myself back into dreams
Where I can control the narrative
And people don't say stupid things.
In this place, I'm not the me that you see,
But someone different, someone better
It's a place where simple me, can simply be.

Sacrifice:
Sometimes I cry, like right now,
When I think about what my family did
For me, so that I could be better.
It's my turn now,
To bear my soul, to bleed for them,
To give them a chance to rest,
As they have given me a chance to rise.

i gave you my all

I stood by your side
as the castle walls crumbled
and your lies were swept away in the tide.

Together in the darkness, we stumbled
but I grasped your hand
and assumed reality would leave you humbled.

But you only knew how to command
so I shut my mouth and let you lead.
I soon came to understand.

You were not above that dreadful deed.
You had no quarrel about cutting our thread
and leaving me for dead.

See, you never learned to not
bite the hand that feeds you.

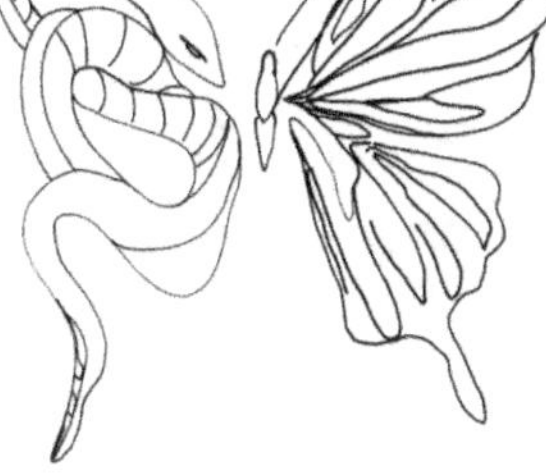

But I rose up from the shallow grave
and on my way to new land,
I found your dismantled crown.

the trenches of your twisted love

My brittle bones break
under pressure
but my heart beats on.

Your words still sting like a slap
but underneath it all
I march on.

Still, you always know how to
ruin me.

A simple flick of the tongue
and guilt fills my lungs.

You wrap your fiberglass love
around my shoulders.

Resignation pricks my skin
and I know:

I'll never be free of you,
                    will I?

blood bond

Your face watches me in the mirror.
But that wasn't all you gave me
was it?

Memories of your manipulation grip me.
Even in adulthood you won't leave me be.

Resentment fuels your ridicule.
Boundaries are broken by your false benevolence.

Guilt-trips fly me to new places.
Places where you punish and penalize me.

I can't stand you.

But I still love you.

What a fucked up way you've made me.

death by narcissist

If the scars you dealt
with your bloody sword
of torment were on
the outside,
I would be more monster than woman.

But you see me that way already?
                    don't you?

Because you mistook my
boundaries
for a slight against your
motherhood.

Because you mistook my
distance
for wishing you out of
existence.

Because you mistook my
tears
for your own far-fetched
fears.

i used to be an optimist

But now I see the world for what
    it is.
I see people for the darkness
    they are.

My father keeps asking
"When did you become a cynic?"
He does not like *this* me.

But *I* do not like that
children cower in corners getting
shot like sheep in schools.

I do not like that
women's wombs are
wielded like weapons.

And, *I* do not like that
politicians problem-solve peace
with penises, piety, and penance.

So, father, hear me when I say:
It is not cynical to cast aside
the rose-colored glasses.

when the lights start to dim

to exist is to cause suffering

Bitter
Sweet
somehow incomplete.

The wind dies down,
Summer saunters in
like the seasons, people leave.

Restless he is
like rustling leaves.
In the end —

all is gone.
Nothing is complete.
Not your last wish
and, certainly,
not the living you leave
behind.

nothing prepared me for this

When the cars have gone silent
and you watch the clock, reminiscent,
don't allow yourself to feel
guilt or regret.

Remind yourself —
this is life;
you did what you could.

And after you call bullshit on that,
after you shout and cry,
take a rest —
you'll need it for what's next.

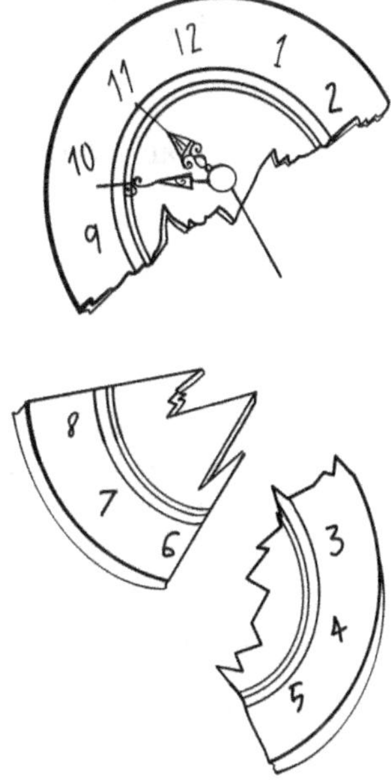

the end foretold

The last breath
brings relief
and grief.

Alone —
a delicate darkness
shrouds you.

I know the phone will ring.
Some poor nurse
to inform of us of your end.

They'll burn your body
for $1250.
That night,
I'll get wasted in your honor
and to bury my:
regrets,
remorse,
resentment.

silence III

Propped up against a pillow
pondering these last days.

I was right about the doom.
You passed alone in a hospital room.

10:47 on Christmas night
we were told you lost your fight.

I knew that it was coming
but it's not easier, just numbing.

We said goodbye three weeks ago
but I still don't have closure, no —

there are things left unsaid...
    forgive me?

ruminations revisited

You once asked me to hand you
your faded little black phone book.
I'd flipped through it absent-mindedly
before asking why so many names were crossed out.

I can still hear your nonchalant voice
telling me those are your dead friends.

I wonder who struck a line
through your name after
that dreadful Christmas.

I wish I could strike
a line through the memories
you left behind.

But your pain and love have
both cornered me.

And your ashes hide in my cabinet
away from sight but never mind.

glassy eyes in my mind

I resented you
for the worlds of pain
you thrashed upon my young soul.

But on a Thursday night
your thin hand was held by mine
as the infection burrowed deep into your lungs.

You were restless and looked at me
with glassy eyes
whispering for your mother.

What a bittersweet end that approached
and we both knew it.

I resented you
but as I watched you cry in your sleep
I knew that I loved you.

And even now as you haunt my
quiet moments and happy memories,
I miss you.

I resented you
but never as much as I resent
the finality of your demise.

how death steals life

I feared Death once.
When I envisioned taking my last breath,
my hands could not still,
my breath, would not even,
and my mind, well,
there was no quiet to be heard.

But Death has visited many times
with watchful, wondering eyes.
Her sinister intentions cannot be cloaked
nor should they be.
She imitates a wildflower
but I find her closer to a rose.

While I feared Death
I forgot to live.
Or, perhaps,
I feared to live.
To be content,
to know love,
to partake in such humanity
is to invite Death.

nightly hauntings

Lights off,
tears running over my lips,
open wounds linger in my soul-deep trough.
Shaking body framed by this bed's grip.

This one is for:
the child ghost
whose open casket
stares back at me.

This one is for:
the naive college girl
whose lips only wanted a taste
not shame and the feeling of disgrace.

This one is for:
the confused boy
whose step-father stomped him
into self-hatred and survival mode.

Lights on,
my love for you is not gone.
You may feel lost now,
but please know,
 you've not lost *me*.

stumbling through the darkness

the coming days

Reach inside —
let me know what you find.

I'll tell you what I found:
misery
and a sense of despair.
Anxiety for the coming days
and what they hold.
A grave emptiness
that I cannot shake.

How do you fill a void
that you never knew existed?

How do you pick yourself up
and find a light to follow?

They tell me to just keep going.
I guess that's worked so far —
if the point was to
lose myself.

stardust

I hate how the
city lights
snuff out the
stars.

In one breath
I feel closer to destiny
than ever,
yet farther in the next.

The agony of knowing that
the beauty I seek is
unreachable and unrecognizable
but its there:

What wouldn't I give
to feel the stars on my skin,
while they obliterate me
— while they make me whole,
Again.

the chase

This pain reflects my inner turmoil;
How can I learn to let go of
the dead?

Dreams and people —
gone all the same.
A lingering, absent-minded pain now resides.

How can I learn to let go of
the love I feel for my loss?

Would it be a lie:
If I said I wanted to remember?
If I said I wanted to wallow?

I feel so far —
suffering is the only way
I belong here.

Maybe I'll stay a little longer.
Let it linger a little more.
Maybe then I'll feel human.

just darkness and me

It used to be that a light somewhere guided me,
But now I feel so damn empty.
It's just darkness and me.

Push and pull—which direction do I go?
I don't know how to choose.

My feet are frozen in sand
And I cannot reach your outstretched hand.

Please somebody help me
Cause I feel it all crashing around me.

Push and pull—which direction do I go?
I don't know what to do.

My legs are weak from the weight
And this storm will not break.

Please somebody help me
Cause I can feel wind scorch my skin.

Push and pull—which direction do I go?
I don't know what more they want from my poor, poor soul.

the danger of desire

It's beautiful up here
among the stars,
as among the stars as one can be
while floating in the space above
Earth but not *in* space.

Oh, so beautiful!
Those little twinkling
balls of flame.
They seem so close,
as if I could reach out
and capture one.

What a shame that would be
to capture
and ruin
what burns so bright.

high performer

There is a loneliness
in looking at your accolades
on the wall.
There is an emptiness
to it all.

I know I should be proud
but these dead trees mean
nothing to me.

And I feel nothing
because of them.

It's like the door to the rest of my days
has been ripped from sight.

All that's left is my
decaying body in a dark room
wondering how to find
my way out.

It's a quarter to 2:06
but my fingers ache to
turn back the clock.

Ache for my youthful innocence.

reminders

Goosebumps on skin
Shivering
Reminds me I'm alive

Chattering teeth bite my tongue
Bleeding
Reminds me I am human

Tears roll down my cheeks
Salty
Reminds me I am vulnerable

Body next to mine
Warmth
Reminds me I am loved

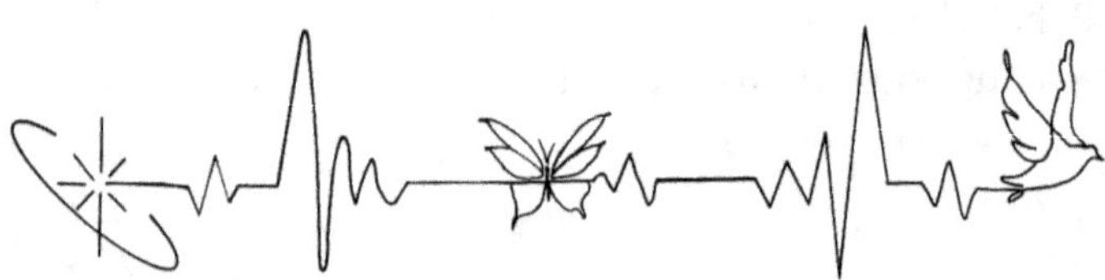

how to feel again

It's easy, I've realized, to shut people out —
even your own self.

It's not hard telling them you're
fine when they ask how you're
doing or crying in the shower
to pretend it didn't happen.

The hard part is
ripping the bandage off your bleeding heart
and feeling.

Feeling the anguish
the loss,
the guilt.

You can repress it, but sooner or
later you a) run out of bandages
or b) need surgery for the hemorrhaging.

feeling the sun on my skin again

that first day

I ran off the plane
searching for your open arms.

Didn't see you standing right there
until you were already holding me.

My muffled laugh vibrated
your hooded chest.

Ain't it funny,
how your smell still lingers like a touch?

You took my luggage to the car
and my cheeks hurt for hours.

I was mesmerized by the deep
color of the English countryside.

But your warm knee next to mine
drew me from my wide-eyed trance.

As the walls of centuries past closed in,
I knew I was finally home.

v. walker

the locket in my heart

You are sunshine
during sorrow.
You are kindness
during madness.

You are the blue
to my skies.
The aloe
for my burns
and the grazing of
the wind when I feel
stuck — unable to bend.

More than a rock,
more than the best...

you are the truest friend,
more than this whole
stupid world could ever comprehend.

oceanic divinity

Ocean eyes
looking into mine.

How divine —
how divine the love is
beneath your eyes.

Tears in flux,
moving against the tide
that tries to hold them back.

But alas
there is no anchor that can withstand
the thrashing,
waves of pain
in those deep, ocean eyes.

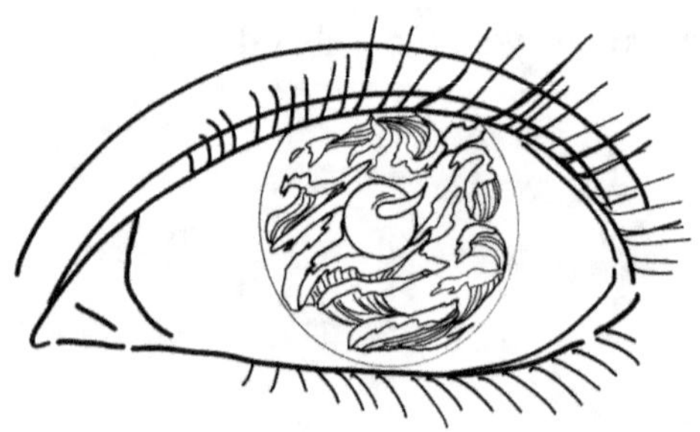

v. walker

the graveyard in your eyes

The starlight bounces off your still face,
closed eyes and breaths so gentle
that I cannot help but wonder
Are you dead?

But those blue eyes startle open
make contact with the sky
and from your lips roll a single sigh.

I envy the graveyard in your eyes.
What would it take for you
to look at me the way you
lose yourself in the dying sky?

if i could see your soul

My eyes wander your seemingly smooth face
as my mind wonders what lies beneath the mask.

If I could see your soul,
would there be layers of pain,
scuffs, scratches, scars to mark what is lost,
particles, patches, pieces to mark what is gained,
would there be anything reminiscent of the man I love
or would your darkness simply consume me?

mysteries of my lover

You fell asleep on the plane
and I admired the sun looking down on your cheeks.

I have no regrets when
it comes to loving you.

I wish I deserved for you to say the same.
I wish I deserved you.

Manipulation lessons from my mother
turn my thoughts into a five-hundred-degree oven.

I've always wondered how you survive a love
that burns you from the inside.

I've always wondered why you stay.

tremors

She wears scars like a crown.
New skin glittering in the sun,
Drawing every pair of eyes to attention,
Not a single hard step is taken around her
For fear that the shaking ground
Will break her
Brittle bones.
But she is not an eggshell to be tread
Upon lightly.

She is a woman who
Loves deeply,
Gives freely,
Survives daily
And embraces the tremors as another obstacle to be overcome.

the only home i need is you

Every day, with you, my love
is an adventure unlike any other.

From spinning atop Warwick Castle's walls
to the burger van in Tesco's parking lot.

My birthday at The Perch in Edinburgh
and walking Victoria Street at 6 am for the perfect photo.

When the Embassy wouldn't let me in
and the London chill bit through my leggings.

The room service we ran up in Turkey
and almost getting stranded in Istanbul's airport.

When you ordered pizza, again, for dessert in Verona
and the Marco Polo gondola ride through Venice.

You know I can't let Mexico go
or the condescending doctor after I broke my elbow.

When we climbed the Eiffel Tower against your will
and gunshots outside our AirBnB kept you up.

That delivery driver in Belgium who rode his scooter
into the hotel lobby
and how you laughed at me for finally speaking French after
we'd left France.

Your tense body slumped over the wheel
as we waited in the Eurotunnel.

French roads at night with no English signs
and that was before you knew you needed glasses.

Those bugs that bit your legs up in Lyon
and the chocolatier who asked how we met.

Swiss mountains surrounded us
and the fresh apple pie our host had made.

Crossing the border into Germany for a sausage
and realizing the world was at our fingertips.

We planned trips spontaneously
even though we were broke.

I worked from the car, trains, hotels, and bars.
We learned about the world and grew closer.

And I decided I never wanted another.
It's always been you, my love.

About the Author

V. Walker is a poet, indie game designer, and avid cookie burner. She is passionate about collecting too many journals and exploring castles. When not writing poetry, you can find her creating interactive fiction (or staring at the "This Is Fine" meme while contemplating the realities of a quarter-life crisis).

Find more of her work:
www.vwpublishing.com
@vwpublishing

Acknowledgements

To my husband, I am eternally grateful for your willingness to always listen and provide honest feedback. You never complain but always listen with an open heart. Thank you for listening, and for loving me.

To the rest of my family and friends, thank you for reading your obligatory copy and supporting me. I love you all a thousand times over.

To my college professors, thank you for believing in me. I'm grateful for your feedback and patience.

And to the readers who don't know me personally but decided to spend their time with *the fragile humans we are,* I can't express my gratitude with words. Ironic, yes. Truthful, also yes. Growing up as an only child, I was armed with a journal early on and found solace in writing. I never stopped.

For a long time, I didn't even think about sharing my work. But then I realized we're all just trying to navigate the contrasting world we share. We're all fragile.

But we're resilient, too.

Thank you. Thank you. Thank you.

-Vi

check out my other work

www.ingramcontent.com/pod-product-compliance
Lightning Source LLC
Chambersburg PA
CBHW070253310726
48976CB00008B/2639